The Jungle Challenge

The Jungle Challenge

Bear Grylls

Illustrated by Emma McCann

 Bear Grylls

First American Edition 2017
Kane Miller, A Division of EDC Publishing

First published in Great Britain in 2017 by Bear Grylls, an imprint
of Bonnier Zaffre, a Bonnier Publishing Company
Text and illustrations copyright © Bear Grylls Ventures, 2017
Illustrations by Emma McCann

For information contact:
Kane Miller, A Division of EDC Publishing
PO Box 470663
Tulsa, OK 74147-0663
www.kanemiller.com
www.edcpub.com
www.usbornebooksandmore.com

Library of Congress Control Number: 2017946253

Printed and bound in the United States of America
6 7 8 9 10

ISBN: 978-1-68464-043-0

To the young survivor
reading this book for the first time.
May your eyes always be wide-open
to adventure, and your heart full
of courage and determination to
see your dreams through.

REACH FOR THE RECORD

Omar's eyes lit up as he spotted the poster on the bulletin board.

"Special prize? That's mine!"

All the activities at camp were listed on the board. Sailing. Night hike. Crazy golf. Horse riding. But it was the brightly colored words next to the "Minds & Muscles Relay Race" that had caught Omar's attention. He picked up the pencil next to the sign-up sheet and wrote his name.

A leader was tidying up the old notices from the board, and she smiled.

"That one's a favorite at every camp. But hang on. You need to say which type of obstacle too."

She tapped the columns next to the names on the sheet. Omar took a closer look.

Do you want to Challenge your MIND

or

Challenge your MUSCLES??

Omar thought. In a normal relay race, each person in a team carries a baton part of the way then hands it over to the next runner. But this one had obstacles and mental challenges too. Which type was for him? *Hmm.*

Sometimes in class, when the teacher asked a question, Omar's mind would go blank. Even just a simple math problem, and the answer would be on the tip of his tongue, but it only came blurting out when the teacher had moved on to another kid. Man, he hated it when that happened. He hated feeling like a loser.

He wasn't going to risk it. He was determined to get that feeling of winning instead. Whatever the cost.

So, he put a check next to "Muscles."

The leader smiled again.

"Well, good luck. There's a special prize for any team that beats the race record."

It was like a hit of adrenaline for Omar. A *record*.

Every year, Omar got the *Guinness World Records* book on his birthday. He loved reading about all the champions. He would flip through it and look at the different records, and choose which ones he was going to beat when he was older.

Omar set off back to his tent feeling pretty excited.

"Definitely going to win that!" he told himself.

Omar played a little game he had made up as he walked through the trees. He would kick a loose pinecone, it would bounce ahead, and then he would kick it again the next time he came up to it, and so on. But the rule was that he couldn't break step, or change direction. Sometimes it would bounce right off the path, so he would have to start with a new cone.

His record so far was kicking the same pinecone four times along the path, before it decided to bounce itself out of play. But this time he got up to five before it went off.

"Score!" he said, pretending to be a sports commentator. "Omar's on top, again!"

Meanwhile he had come out of the trees into the clearing where a five-a-side game was just finishing. Suddenly a girl screamed very loudly. Omar looked over and smiled – one of the girls had accidentally squirted her friend with a bottle of fruit juice.

The look on the wet girl's face was pretty funny.

But he stopped smiling when he saw one of the girls drop the empty bottle of juice. He thought her name was Chloe. Instead of putting the bottle in a trash can, she just chucked it on  the ground as she headed off with her friend.

"Hey!" he called, hurrying after them, but she didn't hear him.

Omar frowned. Annoyed. His mom was always on him to make sure he picked up his litter. How come she could just get away with it?

"Hey, Omar!"

He was distracted by hearing his

7

tentmates, Olly and Jack, call him. So he picked the bottle up and chucked it into the trash can as he headed over to them.

"Hey, guys!" he called. "Guess what I just put my name down for?"

2

MINDS AND MUSCLES

"Um … um … twenty-three … *no*, twenty-two … um … fifteen …"

There were two teams, Yellow and Red. Omar was on the Yellow team.

A boy called Joe was trying to do the second mind obstacle in the race. He had to count backward from fifty, by sevens. A girl called Mia was doing the same for the Reds, and she was slightly ahead. The first mind obstacle had been saying the alphabet backward. Omar was very glad he had signed up for a muscles obstacle.

So far the two teams were neck and neck. Joe and Mia got to the end of their counts almost at the same time, and handed the baton over to the next runners, Sophie and Jacob. The race track twisted and curved through the woods, so everyone else could dash straight to the next obstacle and get there before the runners, to cheer them on.

Next was a muscles obstacle. It was a big sandy pit the runners had to get across by zip line. The two runners appeared around the bend in the track. Jacob was slightly ahead, for the Reds. Sophie was trying hard, but she just wasn't overtaking him.

"Come on, slowpoke!"

The words came out of Omar without

him thinking. He ran alongside her, to shout more. He wanted to get that little extra effort out of her. Sophie just needed to move her feet that little bit faster.

Sophie reached the sandpit just ahead of Jacob. She tucked the baton into her hoodie and leaped onto the zip line. Omar grinned as she shot off. Excellent. His shouting had worked. They might beat the record!

Omar didn't see exactly what happened next, but he almost screamed in frustration when he realized that Sophie had fallen off and the Reds had already handed their baton over.

Fatima, who was next to run for the Yellows, jumped down into the pit to help Sophie.

A leader shouted a warning. "She has

to get to the side first!"

Sophie looked a bit dazed as she picked herself up. Omar felt anger boiling up inside him. By now the Reds had to be something like thirty seconds ahead.

He couldn't help the words that came pouring out as Sophie finally handed the baton to Fatima.

"Can't you even stay on a zip line?"

Omar hurried through the woods to the next obstacle. He was going to be the next runner.

It was another muscles obstacle – a pair of rolling logs. The runners had to get across them without falling off before they could hand over the baton.

Fatima fell off several times. Fortunately Jacob was just as bad. Omar felt anger starting to boil inside him again. How could she not see what to do?

She didn't have to get all the way across. She just had to get far enough to hand him the baton.

"Just run! You don't need to stay on it all the way, just get near enough to me!"

Eventually she got it. Fatima held the baton out ahead of her, and Omar could grab it even though she promptly fell off again. But he didn't care – he was already running.

The two boys pelted through the trees. The Red boy was really fast and just slightly ahead when they got to the next obstacle. They had to crawl through a pair of plastic pipes before handing off.

Omar flung himself forward into his pipe headfirst. He wriggled his way along like a caterpillar, jacking his whole body and banging himself against the side. He was the first out and he thrust the baton at his teammate. It was Chloe, the girl who had dropped the bottle.

"Now, run! *Run!*"

Chloe turned – and tripped. The baton went flying, into the hands of Sophie, who had caught up.

"GET UP!" Omar shouted at Chloe. He was immediately ashamed of himself because he could see that she had hurt herself. But the desire to win was like a raging fire inside him. He couldn't control it. To Omar, winning mattered more than anything.

The Red team's runner, a boy called Charlie, had already disappeared down the track.

Chloe was still clutching her leg. But then Sophie was running with the baton instead. And she was really fast.

Omar got to the finish just in time to see Sophie pull the prize out of a tub full of maggots.

It was like suddenly being able to breathe again. They'd won! They'd won!

Omar was really pleased. But had they beaten the record?

3

LOST IN THE WOODS

"Overall time ..." The leader checked her board and shook her head. "Sorry. Twenty-two seconds off the camp record, I'm afraid."

It was like being socked in the stomach. No record. No special prize.

Well, at least his team had won, thanks to Sophie. Omar thought he should congratulate her. So he went over to her and told her well done, but he couldn't resist grumbling about the missed record.

"Oh, well," Sophie said carelessly. "We did our best, and we won the race."

Omar glared at her. She didn't get it!

"Not the point," he muttered, and he walked away.

"Nice one, Omar!" shouted a cheerful voice.

Olly and Jack were hurrying over.

"Yellows won, right?" Jack said. "That's cool!"

Omar couldn't stand looking at their cheerful, happy faces. No one got it! What's the point of trying so hard if you didn't get the record?

"Kind of," he said through his teeth. "I, uh, just remembered something I have to do, uh, over here."

Omar hurried away quickly before they could ask what the something was. He just wanted to be on his own. When he thought about the last twenty minutes, he felt his toes curl with embarrassment.

Deep down, Omar knew he hadn't been nice. He had shouted at Sophie in the race and then been rude to her afterward.

And then he had brushed his friends off.

But none of them understood what it was like.

"Like a drink, Omar?" said a voice behind him. He turned in surprise. He hadn't noticed anyone following him, but Sophie was offering him a juice carton.

He took it.

"Thanks." He still felt bad about his temper.

"You know ..." she said carefully. "You took the race pretty seriously, didn't you?"

It was like she had pressed a button inside him. A button marked "temper." Omar felt tears of frustration and shame pricking his eyes. Words just came spilling out of him.

"I just like to win. Is that so bad? So why

am I *always* surrounded by slowpokes?!"

He started to walk away before he said something really unkind.

"Hey, Omar?" she called gently. When he looked back, Sophie was holding something out. "I just want to give you this."

He took it out of curiosity.

"Just consider it a gift," she added.

It was a compass. It obviously meant something to her. If there was one thing Omar knew he didn't deserve, it was a gift. And he didn't need a compass. But he didn't want to be even ruder than he had been, so he put it in his pocket.

"Thanks."

She smiled and went back to her friends.

Omar still couldn't face the thought of

mixing with other people, so he headed off on his own.

He didn't really notice which way he was going. If he heard people one way, he went the other.

24

Strange feelings churned inside him, and he just wanted to cry. He was really embarrassed by his behavior. He started to feel warm all over. Really warm. A line of sweat trickled out of his hair and he wiped it away while he thought.

Omar liked camp. He liked the other kids and all the activities. But winning was just so important to him. Coming first. After all, the opposite of winning was losing. And he didn't want to be a loser. Who did?

Sure, Omar knew other people said that doing your best and being kind was more

important. Like Sophie, who didn't seem
to care too much about the special prize.

But how could she think like that?

The frustration boiled up in him.

"Aaargh!!"

Omar swung his fist sideways into the
nearest tree. His hand thudded into the
rough bark and his shout changed into a
loud, *"Owwww!"*

Trees were tougher than they looked.

Omar studied his hand, and drew in his breath with a sharp hiss. He had cut a gash at the base of his little finger and blood was oozing out. It really stung. He felt a bit dizzy and hot all over. His hair was damp with sweat.

"Smart move, Omar," he muttered. "Now you can win a special prize for Kid at camp Who Hurt Himself in the Silliest Way!"

Omar had thought Sophie was pretty pathetic when she fell off the zip line. This was about a hundred times worse.

He needed to get an adult to look at it, so he climbed to his feet.

That was when he realized he had no idea which way to go.

The bushes were thick in every

direction and he was surprised how dark it seemed. And it really was hot.

Why was it so hot all of a sudden?

Omar tried to listen out for the sounds of camp – shouts and laughing and people generally having fun.

Nothing. But there was a lot of strange birdsong, all whoops and whistles.

So, which way should he go?

He might set a record after all – a whole new record, for Kid Who Managed to Get Lost at camp, he thought. *I could do without winning that one, thanks.*

Then he remembered, he *did* have something that could help! He had a compass.

"Thanks, Sophie," Omar said, and he pulled the compass out of his pocket.

But he couldn't remember the layout

of camp. Did he want to go north, south, east or west?

Omar looked at the compass. The dial was turning fast, around and around. And somehow there were five directions on it. So the compass was basically useless. Not much of a gift at all.

Omar rolled his eyes and stuffed it back into his pocket. He needed to get going, and not worry about the silly compass. He picked a direction at random, and started to walk fast.

Big mistake. He seemed to have picked

a path through the thickest bushes there were. The leaves and branches closed around Omar. The farther in he pushed, the harder it got to keep going. The damp air was like a thick blanket wrapped around him. Sweat streamed down his face. He shook his head to get the drops out of his eyes.

The salt in his sweat made the cut in his hand sting. Leaves scraped against his face and scratched the bare skin of his arms and legs.

"This is crazy!" Omar hurled himself forward into the bushes. A forked branch almost jabbed him in the eye.

Then a voice shouted, right behind him.

"Hey, stop *right* there! Don't move a muscle!"

It was a man's voice, and it was filled with urgency and purpose. Omar did what he was told. He paused exactly where he was, with one foot lifted up.

"Stay very still," said the man. "Look about three feet ahead of your left foot."

Omar glanced down – and got a huge shock.

The head of a very large, very vicious-looking snake poked out of the leaves. Its scales were shiny and bright green. Its tongue flicked in and out and its yellow slit eyes were fixed on him.

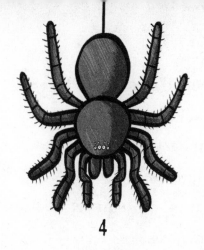

4

MORE HASTE, LESS SPEED

"Good reactions! Now hold tight. Give me a few seconds to help you out," the man behind him said, in a more relaxed manner.

Omar stayed exactly where he was. He balanced on one foot and tried very hard not to fall over. He didn't want to do anything that would upset the snake.

From the corner of his eye, Omar saw a long stick move slowly toward the snake.

"When the snake attacks the stick," said the man, "just walk backward. Straight back. Got it?"

"Straight back. Got it," Omar said. The snake was still staring at him with its yellow eyes.

The stick got to within a few inches of the snake's head. The snake suddenly struck at it in a blur of movement.

"Now!" the man said. Omar flung himself backward. As he put as much distance between himself and the snake as possible, something caught Omar's heel and he tripped. He landed on his back with a thud that knocked the breath out of him. But at least he was out of the bushes.

He peered back
quickly to see if there was
anything bright green and scaly coming
at him.

But it had disappeared into the bushes.
Gone.

Omar picked himself up and got his
first look at the man. He had dark hair
that was damp with sweat, like Omar's,
but he still managed to look fresh and
cheerful. Despite the heat he wore a
long-sleeved shirt and pants, both made
of a tough-looking material. He had a
backpack, and he was leaning on the
long, thick stick he had used on the
snake. A canvas scabbard on his belt
held a machete – a big knife with a wide,
flat blade.

35

"Who are you?" Omar asked.

The man smiled.

"I'm Bear – I'm going to guide you out of here. And *that* was a highly poisonous blue temple viper."

"Poisonous!" Omar exclaimed.

"Highly poisonous. As a general rule, the more colorful a reptile is, the more likely it is to be dangerous. The color is a warning to other animals. And that one, remember, was really bright green. Its venom would have turned your blood into a big lump of black pudding."

Omar's mouth hung open.

"There are poisonous snakes at camp? We've got to warn people! Someone could tread on one."

"Well …" Bear started to say, but Omar didn't stop to hear the rest. He hurried off in the opposite direction.

"Hey! You need to slow down," Bear called after him.

"You don't understand!" Omar shouted. "These woods are full of kids …"

He stumbled as something caught his leg. A vine covered with thorns had wrapped around his knee. He had just walked into it without looking. Omar tried to tug his leg free, but it only seemed to get tighter.

"Watch yourself, buddy ..." Bear began, but Omar wasn't listening. He pulled his leg out with an extra hard effort and scraped his shin. His bare skin glistened with sweat and it made the scrape sting twice as hard.

Omar ignored the pain, and Bear, and hurried on. The branches ahead seemed to be pushing him back. Thorns came straight at his face and he flinched. He yelped as he saw a massive hairy spider, the size of his hand, right in front of him. Then, finally, he stopped.

"Hey, take it steady," Bear said gently, arriving behind him. "If you want to survive and get out of here alive, then listen to me and slow it all down. You're going to need to use your brain as well as your brawn. Okay?"

Omar followed reluctantly as Bear led the way carefully.

Bear constantly poked his stick into the undergrowth or prodded lumps on the ground. Everywhere Bear went, he held the stick in front of him.

"For a start," he said over his shoulder, "always look where you're going, every step of the way. We are always listening and observing. And we use a stick to go first, so that if we upset anything it attacks the stick, not us. I'll cut one for you."

Omar remembered how close he had gotten to the snake's fangs without noticing, and he shuddered. *Okay, maybe this guy does know what he's doing*, he thought.

After a few minutes they came to a clearing. Bear turned to face Omar, and smiled.

"See?" He held his hands out. "More haste, less speed. Go steady and don't rush. That's the first rule for survival in a place like this ... and for life, really."

Omar screwed his nose up, puzzled.

"What do you mean, survival? We're only ..."

Omar looked around him. He had been going to say they were only in the woods around camp.

41

He *was* surrounded by trees and bushes, but they were very different from the woods he was thinking of. Bigger, for a start. Much bigger.

Omar craned his head back. The trees had to be sixty feet high, or more. Up above, their thick branches tangled together and blocked out the sky.

And every space – on the tree trunks, on the ground – was filled with plants. Thick, leafy vines wrapped around everything.

His feet sank into a thick carpet of rotting leaves.

And now that he noticed that, he noticed more things. There weren't just a few birds singing.

The trees were alive with a hundred different birds and a thousand different insects.

The air was so hot it was like trying to breathe with his head in a bath.

"Welcome to the jungle," Bear said.

5

NAVIGATING NATURE

"Where are we? Where's camp?" Omar asked.

"Wherever it is, we'll need to get out of the jungle first to find it," said Bear. "Are you ready for a *real* adventure?"

Omar thought for a moment. Maybe when they got back they'd be famous and get awarded a special prize. They might even make it into the *Guinness World Records* …

"Sure. I'm in," Omar said. He tugged

at his T-shirt, which was stuck to his skin with sweat. And he rubbed his hurt hand. It didn't sting anymore, but it throbbed a lot. "How long will it take to get back?"

"Everything here takes some time – and some care." Bear looked him up and down. "You were in quite a hurry back there. Out here, if we cut corners, we die."

"But I like to move fast!" Omar replied.

Bear laughed. "So do I. But if you want to move fast, then first you have to learn how to move safely. Anyway, we'll get to that. First up, tell me your name."

"Omar."

"Well, Omar, we'll set off soon. But not like that. Shorts and T-shirts aren't for the jungle. Everything scratches and scrapes, so you want as little exposed

46

skin as possible."

Bear rummaged in his
backpack, and pulled
out a pair of boots,
followed by a shirt
and pants of the same
tough material that Bear was wearing.

"Try these on for size, and I'll go and
get something for that cut of yours."

Omar pulled on the new clothes
and immediately felt better. The
tough material would
stand up to the jungle's
thorns and spikes, and
soak up the sweat that
covered his skin. The
boots gripped his feet
and kept him steady
on the spongy ground.

47

He looked at the pile of his old clothes and wondered what to do with them. He started to fold them up carefully.

Bear came back and saw what he was doing.

"Good job. Look after your things and they will look after you. Put them in this," he said, opening his backpack. "And look, I also got you some of nature's antiseptic." Bear held out a handful of brownish-red berries. "Rattan berries."

Bear pressed his palms together and rubbed hard to mangle the berries into a thick red paste.

"Let's see that cut?"

Omar cautiously held his hand up. Bear dabbed a finger into the paste and smeared it on. The throbbing turned to stabbing. Omar yelped.

"That really hurts! It feels like an army of ants chewing on my hand."

Bear smiled, and kept rubbing.

"That means it's working. You know, in some places they use bullet ants to clamp a wound together instead of stitches. Their jaws are about half an inch wide. So you hold the ant with the

jaws on either side of the wound, make it bite you, then you twist its body off and leave its head in your skin." He paused. "Consider yourself lucky we have a bandage!"

Omar imagined a row of dead ant heads on his hand, holding the sides of the cut together. Okay, maybe he could take a little stinging from the berries after all.

Bear washed the paste away with water from a canteen, and wrapped the wound in a clean bandage from a box in

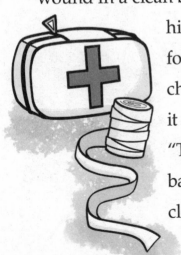

his backpack. Next he folded a red-and-white check bandana and tied it around Omar's hand. "This will protect the bandage and keep it clean," Bear explained.

"That's really important in the jungle."

Last of all, Bear used his machete to cut Omar a stick like his. He lopped off a long, thin branch from a tree, and sliced off the leaves. Then they took a couple of mouthfuls of water from Bear's canteen, and set off.

It was like before, when Bear had gotten Omar out of the bushes. He didn't walk in a straight line. He ducked and dodged, swerved and sidled. And everywhere he went, his stick went first. Omar did his best to copy him, without his stick getting stuck in the thick tangle of branches and pulled out of his hands.

"This is impossible," Omar said out loud.

Bear answered without looking around.

"Patience and perseverance are key in the jungle. Don't rush and never give up. And learn from how the animals move," Bear said. "Imagine you're back at home on a busy Saturday. You're trying to walk down the street and so is everyone else. Do you walk in a straight line?"

Omar thought. He knew exactly what the weekend shopping crowd was like when it was busy. Everyone was bigger than him, so all he could do was shuffle along and look for gaps.

"No. I guess I have to move around a bit to get between people."

"And sometimes you have to get over to one side of the sidewalk to keep going, right?" Bear said. "Maybe someone suddenly stops to talk on their phone, so you have to step around them?"

"Sure." Omar had never really thought about it before, but that was exactly what he did. "I'll see someone take the phone out of their pocket, so I know they're going to stop in just a moment, so I can kind of dodge them in advance."

Bear nodded.

"Well, it's the same thing here. You have to anticipate. That's what the tigers and leopards do. They consider every move, and go silently, stealthily through the undergrowth. That way they move swiftly and efficiently." He paused to look around.

"In the jungle your mind is

never in neutral – you need to be alert to danger and to opportunities. Learn to look ahead, see? It comes with practice." He pointed with the stick. "Maybe it all looks the same to you right now, but I can see that right *here* are two bushes growing together, so we can push our way between them …"

And they did.

"And now I can see that the jungle looks darker ahead on our right than on our left. And that's because the ground starts to rise there. So we go this way, and follow the low ground …"

And that was how it went. Omar and Bear pushed on through

the jungle. Whenever Omar saw Bear change direction, he tried to work out what Bear had seen to make him do it. But he couldn't. In fact, if anything, he reckoned Bear was holding back because he didn't think Omar could keep up.

Well, Omar would show him. He'd had at least ten minutes to get used to it. They could do this a whole lot quicker if he went ahead.

Look, there it was – a gap between two trees, plain as day. Omar quickly pushed ahead of Bear to get through it first.

Just then, something seized his foot and stopped him dead. The rest of his body, though, kept going. The ground then rushed up to meet him, and before he could do anything he had planted his face in the soft, rotting leaves.

Omar lay there for a moment and spat out some twigs. He felt absolutely ridiculous.

"You okay?" Bear helped him back up. "Take it steady, remember?"

Omar stood on one foot carefully, to check that it wasn't hurt. Nope – the only thing hurt was his pride.

"I'll be all right," he grumbled.

"Come on, then ..."

So Omar followed behind Bear, still seething with impatience but trying not to push too far or too fast.

Every fifteen minutes or so, they took a drink from Bear's canteen, but only for a few moments before Bear would push them ever onward.

Finally, Bear called a stop after a couple of hours.

"You hungry?" he said. "I know I am."

"Totally!" Omar agreed eagerly.

Bear swung his backpack off and left it

on a log. The log looked rotten and large chunks of it had half fallen off. Omar expected Bear to open up the backpack and get some food out.

But instead, Bear jammed the tip of his blade into the bark of the log. A piece as long as Omar's forearm came away easily.

"Here's lunch!" Bear said with a wry smile.

Omar craned his neck forward with horror, and stared at a mass of enormous wriggling grubs.

6

GRUBS UP

Bear picked up one of the grubs, which looked like lots of bluish-white plastic rings stuck together. It was as thick as one of his fingers, but curled up tight and wriggling. He pulled it out straight and, in front of Omar's astonished eyes, put most of it into his mouth and bit hard.

"You're eating a *maggot!*" Omar said, horrified.

"A grub actually," Bear corrected him with a smile. "Maggots are baby flies, grubs are baby beetles. And there's more protein in one of these than in the same weight of beef." He picked one up and handed it over. "Give it a try. Don't eat the head. But the rest is fine."

Omar took it between his thumb and forefinger and studied it with dread. But Bear had done this, and he seemed to know what he was doing. And Omar

never backed down from a challenge. So he closed his eyes, put it in his mouth, and bit hard.

It was like eating a sausage full of snot. When his teeth bit through the surface there was an explosion of goo inside his mouth. He made a face, then did all he could to swallow it.

"Delicious," he gasped.

Bear chuckled. He had gone over to inspect something the size of several soccer balls that was stuck to one side of a tree trunk. It was brown and knobbly and it looked like a massive scab on the bark.

He talked as he pulled out his machete.

"The general rule is avoid anything that's brightly colored, or hairy, or that has black dots under its skin. And give them a sniff before they go in your mouth. If there's anything that's like peaches or almonds, drop them immediately and wipe your fingers. They might smell amazing, but they have cyanide in them. Extremely poisonous. In fact, deadly. But these are fine …"

As he said "these," Bear stabbed his machete into the lump on the tree. When he pulled it out, it was covered with tiny scurrying insects like pale-white beetles.

"These might be more to your taste," Bear suggested. He scooped up several of the critters by rubbing his finger along the blunt edge of the blade. Then he popped them into his mouth. "Termites. Delicious."

He offered Omar the machete, flat side up. It still had termites on it. Omar steeled himself, then ran his finger along like Bear had, avoiding the sharp edge of the blade.

"Eat them quick before they crawl off," said Bear. "They'll get into your hair, into your ears and nose, even under your clothes and down your pants – all places you *really* don't want insects."

Omar quickly sucked his finger. For a moment he felt the termites tickling his tongue and then they were gone. He  had to admit they tasted better than the grubs. More like an old lemon or orange that had gone stale. He was just going to try some more when

a movement caught
the corner of his eye.

He stiffened and
froze as something
much larger moved in
the bushes. It was long, and round, and
scaly. Omar strained his eyes without
moving his head.

"A ... a snake ... over there ..." he
whispered.

Bear didn't make any sudden moves.
He followed the direction of Omar's
eyes.

Then, in the blink of an eye, Bear put
his machete down and dived into the
bush headfirst.

There was a burst of activity behind
the leaves.

"Not a snake!" Bear shouted.

The branches shook and the whole bush quivered as Bear struggled with ... whatever it was. He backed out of the bush, bent over, with both hands stretched out in front of him. They were wrapped around the tail of a very ugly brown-and-white lizard, which was the size of Omar's arm. It twisted and turned in Bear's hands, trying to snap at his arms while Bear held it a safe distance away from him.

"Well spotted, Omar," Bear said, working hard to control it. "It's a monitor lizard. Or, out here, survival food."

He held the lizard at arm's length with one hand, dangling it by its tail. It still tried to bite him, but it couldn't make itself twist that far.

Bear moved his hand down behind its neck, held the lizard down, grabbed the machete off the ground and swiftly dispatched it. It was all over in a second.

"We thank the jungle for the food, and then we move on. This will give us vital energy when we stop tonight," Bear said.

"We need to make good use of what the jungle provides if we want to survive."

Omar's mind spun.

Bear then sawed off a chunk of the termite nest with his machete, and knocked it free of termites before he put it in his backpack with the lizard.

"This'll come in handy later," Bear said. "It's digested wood so it'll burn nicely."

It took a moment to put two and two together.

"Hang on – digested?" Omar said. He knew what happens to food once it's been digested. "You mean it's …"

"One hundred percent termite poop," Bear agreed, smiling. "Come on. We've got a couple of hours left before we need to set up our camp, so let's use them."

They pressed on through the jungle.

Omar forced himself to go at Bear's pace because he remembered what had happened the last time he tried to go it alone.

On top of his impatience, Omar was also growing thirsty, though Bear made sure they took regular drinks from his canteen. Then he heard something familiar.

"Is that water?" Omar asked. His eyes couldn't see any difference between leaves, but his ears could pick out the sound of trickling through the constant background racket of birdcalls and whooping monkeys.

"Good job, Omar. You're listening to what's around. Becoming a survivor, eh?" Bear replied with a smile. "This is just what we need to fill up our canteens."

Bear pushed a branch aside, then knelt down. It was then that Omar realized they were standing on the edge of a stream. It was only about three feet across. Both banks were overgrown so you couldn't see the water until you were right on top of it.

"I could certainly use a drink," Omar said happily. Without a pause he knelt down next to Bear and scooped up some water with his hands. He brought it up to his lips …

"Wait, Omar! *STOP!*"

7

DEATH BY DIARRHEA

Bear stopped Omar from drinking just in time.

"We have no idea what's in that water!" he said seriously. "Clear water doesn't mean clean water. There's a jungle full of bugs, poop, dead animals, parasites … you name it. And all of it could be in this stream," Bear told him. "Just one upset stomach, just one attack of diarrhea, can knock us right out of the game. We have to lead with our brains first, remember?"

Omar nodded.

"Out here, if you are sick and your body loses water – if you get dehydrated – then traveling in this heat and humidity would become nearly impossible. You see how one small sip can determine if you live or die?"

Omar turned pale at the thought of death by diarrhea. "I, uh, didn't realize."

"Being first won't do you any good if you are dead," Bear said. "The best way to be safe is to boil the water, but when we're on the move ..." He pulled a small bottle from his backpack with a smile and squeezed a couple of drops into the canteen.

"Iodine," Bear said. "It'll make the water taste weird, but in a few minutes we'll have fresh, clean water to drink."

After five minutes, the drops had done their work in the canteen and Bear and Omar both drank from the canteen. Bear was right about the taste – it was terrible and it smelled like a hospital. But it was clean.

Omar was surprised when Bear called a halt soon after that in a clear space.

"That was quick. There's still daylight left."

"There is," Bear agreed, "but it's no good rushing on without thinking, and then regretting it later. We have to make camp before it gets dark. In the jungle, once the sun goes down it gets pitch-black in minutes. We have to be prepared."

"Like the Scouts?" Omar asked with a smile. "Be prepared. Their motto, right?"

Bear smiled. "Right!" He looked around.

"Look! There's useful bamboo here, and –" He pointed up. "See how thin the trees are up there? It means there's less chance of something falling on us during the night. So many jungle injuries happen that way – from falling dead wood. Crazy, eh?"

Omar thought for a moment. "I suppose I thought the animals were the most dangerous thing in the jungle, not falling branches."

"Well, the monkeys often disturb the branches, and then the dead wood falls to the ground. So I guess it's the animals *and* the wood!"

"So, basically, the whole place is dangerous?" Omar replied.

"I guess so. Unless you know how to handle the dangers. And you're learning, Omar. It's good."

Omar smiled back at Bear.

"And the thing about survival," Bear added, "is that we never stop learning. The jungle will always teach us a new lesson if we are calm enough, quiet enough and curious enough to hear it."

Bear pulled out his machete and lopped a branch off a bush. He handed it to Omar, and pointed at the ground.

"Now, first job is to sweep this bit of ground clear. Sweep up the leaves and we sweep up the creepy-crawlies with them, so then we can sit or sleep there."

While Omar swept, Bear built a fire. Underneath the rotting leaves on the ground, Omar was surprised to find clumps of leaves that were bone-dry – the top layer had kept the rain off them.

Bear made a small pile of these dry leaves and arranged sticks and logs on top. Then he struck together two pieces of metal he took off a chain around his neck. Sparks flew and the fire quickly started to burn.

Next, Bear used his machete to sharpen a length of wood, which he stuck in the ground. Then he pulled the dead lizard out of his backpack and carefully cut its front open with the tip of the blade.

"You have to make sure you don't puncture the guts, or the acid just spills out and spoils everything …"

Bear stuck his hand in and worked it around a bit, before pulling out a lump of meat the size of a golf ball. It was smooth and dark rusty brown.

"This is the liver," Bear said. "Very rich in iron and nutrients – and also pretty tasty once we've cooked it. Beats beetle grubs, anyway."

He skewered the liver on the sharp stick.

"What else can we eat from the lizard?" Omar asked.

"This." Bear set about slicing

off the lizard's tail, cutting through the leathery skin. The tail came off with a few machete strokes. "It's mostly meat, and this skin's almost fireproof, so we can cook the whole thing as it is. Then we'll just peel the skin off once it's cooked."

Bear set the liver on a skewer over the flames, and carefully placed the tail on top of the fire. It only took a few minutes for cooking smells to fill the air and Omar's stomach started to rumble.

"Will it take long?" Omar asked.

"Patience, Omar! Before we can eat we need to make somewhere to sleep, and for that we're going to need vine," Bear said. "Lots of it. Like this." He pulled at a vine that clung to a nearby trunk. It was smooth and as thick as his finger, and it reminded Omar of electric cable.

Omar couldn't yet see what Bear had in mind, but he got busy, gathering up clumps of vine. He had to really yank it free of the trees and soon his arms ached

He couldn't use the machete because Bear was attacking the bamboo with it.

"You've seen scaffolding outside buildings?" Bear asked. "Well, bamboo is the scaffolding of the jungle. Light, strong and straight."

The bamboo grew higher than Bear's head, in knobbly poles that were as thick as Omar's arms. Bear chopped the poles into three-foot-long lengths, and he used Omar's vine to tie them together. First he tied six pieces into two frames shaped something like giant letter As. The crosspieces were about twelve inches off the ground.

"What are you making?" Omar asked.

"This is going to be a sleeping frame. It'll keep us off the jungle floor, out of range of anything crawly or slithery. And it'll keep us dry when it rains – which it will, believe me."

By now Omar had gathered all the vine that Bear needed, so Omar was put on cooking duty. He had to keep turning the liver and the tail so that they cooked evenly. The smell of cooking meat made him really hungry.

Bear tied more vine around and around the two long bottom poles on the sleeping frame. Eventually he had made

a loose, baggy net between them out of the vines, like a hammock.

"Now can we –" Omar bit his tongue before he said "eat" because he could see that Bear wasn't finished. He almost squeaked with impatience.

Patience ... he remembered.

Omar smiled to himself. If he had learned anything on this journey so far, it was that he *really* didn't want to be lying on the jungle floor in the dark with all those snakes and bugs around. He reckoned this was one job that was definitely worth doing properly and carefully.

Bear cut bundles of long, thin palm leaves to lay down on the vine net.

"These are our mattress, so we can lie on the vines without them cutting into us."

The last touch was to tie palm leaves along the top pole on the frame so that they hung down on either side of it, like a roof.

Omar looked at the leaves with interest. They weren't flat; they were shaped like Vs, and Bear had set them all up so that they pointed downward.

Omar suddenly realized what they were for.

"To catch the rain?"

"You got it! This is a rain forest, so that means rain. The water will run straight off and into these – lovely fresh water."

Bear set his almost empty canteen at the end of one of the leaves, and he put chunks of hollow bamboo under the others. When it rained, they would fill up.

Finally, Bear jammed the lump of termite nest onto a stick, and set fire to it. Smoke from the burning termite poop drifted over their small camp. It was sharp and caught the back of Omar's nose.

"That'll keep the bugs away," Bear said. "Now, let's eat. I don't know about you, but I'm starving."

8

NEVER SMILE AT A CROCODILE

Omar woke up during the night and heard what sounded like all the rain in the world falling on them in the dark.

He barely dared to move. The rain sounded like a wild animal. The normal night sounds of the jungle – all those chirping and buzzing insects, and squawks and shrieks from creatures he couldn't see – were gone. They couldn't compete with the roar of a thousand tons of water falling every second onto every leaf and twig around him.

He was still more or less dry on the sleeping frame, protected by the roof of leaves Bear had put up over them. Bear had said there would be rain and it wouldn't last for long. He was right on both counts.

As the sound began to slacken, Omar felt his eyes growing heavy again. By the time the rain had stopped, Omar was asleep again.

The next morning the jungle was full of steam. The background noise of birds and monkeys was back to normal. Bear's canteen was full to the brim with fresh rainwater, and there was plenty leftover in the bamboo pots to drink and wipe themselves clean of sweat and grime before they set off.

Bear checked the cut on Omar's hand and changed the bandage. Then he retied the red-and-white bandana over it, and they picked up their sticks and off they went.

Even though Omar was drenched in sweat, he also felt pretty good. To his surprise, he was getting used to walking in the jungle. A good night's sleep had helped his brain sort it all out. The thickness of the plants started to make sense. He could make out the shades and shadows that showed their depth, and the best way around them. He could sense when the ground was going to fall or rise, so he could head in the best direction.

Now he was starting to see why Bear took the route he did, and he could see why they needed to take it steady. *At jungle speed.*

After a while Omar could see that the canopy of leaves over to their right looked thinner.

"Is it lighter over there?" Omar asked.

The day before, he wouldn't have noticed. Leaves were just leaves back then – something that got in his way. But now that he was getting used to the jungle he could see that where he was looking more light was getting through. And that meant there was open space ahead.

Bear smiled.

"It does. Let's check it out."

A few minutes later they stood on the bank of a river. It was about one hundred fifty feet wide, and the water was dark brown, like cold tea. A floating log showed how fast the river was flowing. It was going at the kind of speed Omar could just about manage if he walked as fast as he could.

"Now, that is good news," Bear said. "All rivers go somewhere."

"Where does this one go?"

"I don't know – but if we follow it, we'll get to a village or town eventually." Bear stood with his hands on his hips and stared across the

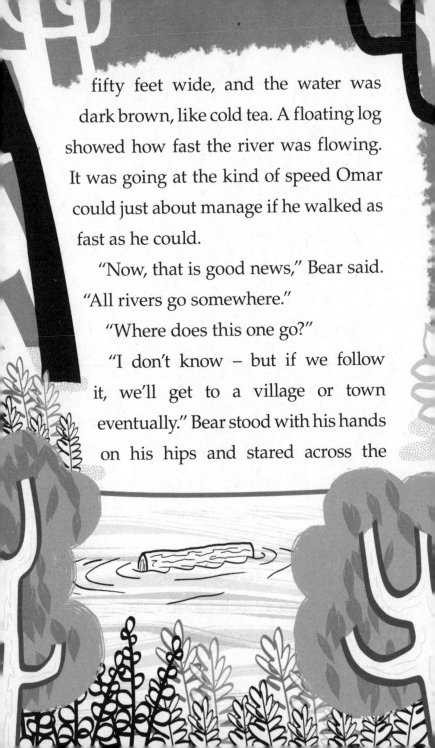

water. His expression was thoughtful and maybe a bit worried.

"Is there a problem?" Omar asked.

"It's much easier going on the far bank. Look. See how the riverbank extends out into the water all the way downstream? But this side is all dense jungle." Bear paused, as if considering. "I think it is going to be worth it to attempt to cross the river and continue downstream from the other side. You good with that? Can you swim?"

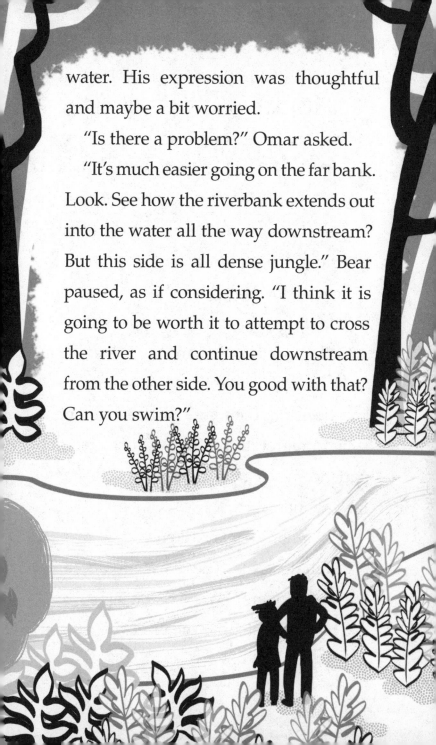

Omar looked at the far bank. He had swum fifty meters at school, no problem. He had the badge on his trunks. He was about to say, "You bet! Let's go!" but then he noticed how Bear was taking it slow. "I guess we should be careful about crossing?" he said instead.

Bear nodded silently.

"Act in haste, repent at leisure, eh?"

"What does that mean?"

"It means if you rush in and make a bad decision, then you will have a long time to regret it! In other words, a bit of patience never hurt anyone. Let's watch for a while."

"For what?" Omar asked.

"Well, let's see. These waters hide all sorts of dangers ..."

They sat, watching the river.

Soon, a group of monkeys came down to the far bank. They had dark fur and their arms were longer than their bodies.

They chatted and hooted among themselves and drank from the water …

Just then, the water exploded suddenly in a cloud of white spray. Something dark and deadly moved within it. The monkeys screamed and screeched and fled – all except one.

The monkey was caught in the jaws of a nine-foot-long reptile. Omar stared in horror. The monster's skin was knobbly and dark, the exact color of the water. It slid back under the surface, still with the monkey in its mouth, and disappeared.

"Move back from the water, Omar," Bear said. "No sudden movements."

They walked backward for a few feet. There was no more sign of the creature.

"That was one big crocodile!" Omar exclaimed.

"Technically it was one big black caiman." Bear didn't stop looking around. "They're native to this part of the world – closely related to crocs and alligators. They're river animals, designed to blend in. They can hold their breath for up to forty-five minutes and swim without a

ripple. So now you see why we waited."
He paused. "Remember, instinct is the
inner voice you should trust. Okay. We
won't cross here. Let's fight smart and
stick to battles we can win."

They trekked together along the
riverbank, keeping a few feet back from
the water. If the vegetation by the river
grew too thick, Bear pulled back even
farther.

"You've seen how well they can hide,"
he said. "A nice thick clump of bushes
is all they need. Caimans have an attack
zone of about six feet – on land. If we stay
farther away than that, we're probably
safe."

"What about in the water?" Omar asked.

"In the water, they'll come for you
whatever. As far as they're concerned,

the water is theirs. So, we'll cross when we come to a nice straight bit, where we can see as far along the river as possible in both directions."

They followed the river until they got to a place where Bear felt it would be safest to cross. The river was about sixty feet wide. Both of them kept their eyes peeled for anything long and scaly, as Bear got closer to the edge of the water.

"Keep an eye on the surface," he said, and he used his stick to hit the water several times. Omar ran his eyes back and forth along the river. Nothing popped up to see what the disturbance was – as far as Omar could tell.

"Okay," Bear said. "We'll wait fifteen minutes and scan the water for bubbles. Those are the telltale mark that a caiman is below the surface. Then, if all is clear, we will cross."

After fifteen minutes they had seen no bubbles. Omar looked at Bear.

"Shall we maybe wait a bit longer?" he asked with a worried expression. "Patience is good, isn't it?"

Bear kept looking at the water.

"We have been patient and now is the time to be brave. It's as good as it's going to get. Time to get ready ..."

Bear stood up and started to use his stick to demonstrate how to cross. He stood so he was leaning on it, with his legs apart.

"You don't know how deep the river gets, or what the bottom will be like, and the current will always try to knock you over. So, use this as a third leg. Every time you move one foot, make sure your other foot and the stick are planted on the riverbed. Don't move your stick without both your feet being secure."

Omar hadn't realized crossing the river would be such a challenge. He nodded nervously. There was a whole new set of rules to learn.

"And above all ..." Bear began.

Omar finished for him. "Don't hurry, take it steady!"

Bear grinned and nodded, and led the way into the water.

9

PART OF THE JUNGLE

The water quickly gurgled into Omar's boots, then felt its way up his legs. It was cool and refreshing, for about a second. Then Omar could feel it tugging at him. It wanted to sweep him away. The bottom of the river was soft and slimy, and it was hard for his boots to get a grip. He jammed the stick into the riverbed with every step to give himself some extra hold.

The water kept on rising as they got

farther out. Knees, hips, stomach ...
The higher it got, the more it wanted
to knock him over. He set his eyes on
the far bank and trudged on. It was so
tempting just to chuck the stick away
and try to wade faster. His mind was
telling him, *Ignore the law of the jungle
and just swim for it.*

But Omar knew if he stopped doing
the river-crossing technique, then the
water would just take him. Sure, he
could swim for the bank and get there
eventually – but he would be swept
downstream, and then what might
happen? He remembered that caiman,
and how invisible it had been right up
until the last moment ...

He needed to stick to the plan.

Omar shifted his bandaged hand

to the top of the stick to keep it out of the water, and kept going. He started to breathe heavily. It was impossible to hurry, even if he'd wanted to now.

"Keep going, Omar," Bear said, turning to look at him. "Slow and steady, but keep going. You'll need to find that inner determination if we're going to get across this safely. You can do it, Omar!"

More than halfway across, Omar finally felt the water start to give. It was getting lower. His legs were aching, but he didn't give up or stop trying. He still took every step just as carefully as before, even when the water was down to his knees and he was splashing through the shallows. His tired legs wobbled with the effort.

Finally, Bear gave him a hand up onto

the far bank. He grinned down at him.

"You couldn't have done that yesterday. You hadn't learned jungle discipline and determination." He paused. "Or jungle humility," he added with a smile. "I'm impressed, buddy."

Omar laughed. "I guess not –"

But Bear was looking over the top of his head, back at the river. His face suddenly changed abruptly and he gave Omar a violent shove.

"Up that tree! Run!"

The ache in Omar's legs vanished and he ran at top speed for the tree that Bear had pointed at. Bear grabbed Omar around the waist and boosted him up. Omar gripped the nearest branch with both hands and swung his legs up. With a bit of wriggling he hauled himself up.

Meanwhile Bear had shinnied up the trunk and sat behind him.

A caiman was coming across the river like a small torpedo. Its eyes, sticking out of the water, made a small bow wave.

Omar gasped. "How fast can they go?"

"Up to twenty miles per hour. That's faster than me or you!"

The caiman hit the bank and kept going. Massive claws the size of a man's hand dug into the mud as it hurled itself onto the land. It slowed down as it strolled over to the tree. It seemed to be swinging its hips as it walked, like it didn't have a care in the world.

I can wait, it seemed to say, as it lay down beneath them. It knew they weren't going anywhere.

Omar gazed with fascination at the killing machine below. It was longer than Bear would be if he lay down next to it. Its scales were as big as both his hands if he clasped them together. Its massive mouth was clamped shut, but pointed teeth still jutted past its lips.

"They can stand on their back legs," Bear said. "Keep your feet up and work your way back here."

Omar carefully wriggled his way back along the branch. He and Bear sat side by side with their backs to the trunk.

"How long do we wait?" Omar asked.

"As long as it takes. Eventually it will go for something easier to catch – I hope."

Eventually! Omar thought. *What good was eventually?*

But once again, he made himself stop thinking like that. It wasn't helpful. This was the jungle. Things took as long as they took, and that was all there was to it. Setting records would have to wait for a day when there wasn't a caiman smacking its chops a couple of feet below him.

Bear untied the bandana to check the bandage on Omar's hand, and nodded in satisfaction at the way the cut was healing.

"It just takes a bit of time – like everything else," he said, and grinned at him.

Omar felt a strange, warm glow inside him. It was a feeling of peace. He realized that he couldn't control everything. He was simply part of the jungle, and he needed to respect its rhythm. Some things he could do – like look after

himself by staying in the tree. Some things he couldn't. And in those cases there was no point fretting about them.

He closed his eyes.

Then something hit his head and his eyes flew open. He twisted around to see what it had been. The world shifted.

"Hey!"

His arms and legs flailed as he tried to get a grip, but he could feel himself falling …

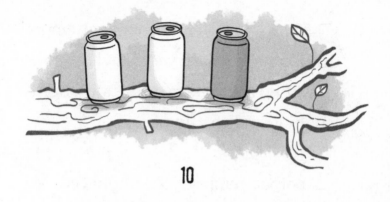

10

SHOOTING GALLERY

Omar struggled to sit up in a sudden panic, thinking of teeth and enormous jaws. But there was no sign of the caiman.

He was lying in a mass of leaves and branches that wanted to tangle him up. And there it was again. *Bop.* Something hit his head.

He looked around for Bear. He wasn't there.

And where was the caiman?

Next to him were a couple of empty drink cans. It wasn't very jungly.

And he could hear the sound of girls laughing and chatting.

Zing. Bop.

Another empty can bounced off Omar's shoulder. He looked up. There was a branch just above him, with a couple more cans perched on it.

"Come on, we should be going," said a girl's voice.

"One more …" said another.

Zing.

Omar saw a rubber band zip past the branch.

Bop.

A shooting gallery.

Omar clambered to his knees and stared over the branch. A group of three

girls were walking away. They hadn't noticed him, but he recognized them all from camp.

And that was where he now was. He looked around him.

The trees were all a normal size. He could see the sky. It wasn't incredibly steamy or hot. And there was no sign of Bear. Or the caiman.

One of the girls was Chloe, the one who had chucked the plastic bottle on the ground earlier. And it didn't look like she was going to pick up these cans either.

Omar pushed himself to his feet. He looked back at the bent branches where he had been lying. Wow. He remembered getting lost after the race. He must have had a little nap and had a really weird dream.

But it had been a good one. He felt so much happier than before.

Omar picked up all the cans and rubber bands he could find before he headed slowly back to join everyone else. There was no rush.

Omar grinned. Bear would be pleased!

But as he walked, Omar remembered how he had acted during the race, and afterward. Had it really been so important to him, setting a new record and winning at any cost? He had made a real fool of himself, especially with Sophie. He should apologize.

When he got back to the clearing everyone else was still chatting and laughing. He saw Sophie over on the other side, though she didn't notice him. Omar started toward the trash cans to get rid of the cans and rubber bands. The pile in his arms was teetering, and he had to speed up. The pile collapsed just as he reached the trash and he aimed the

cans so that most of them fell right in.

But one of the rubber bands caught on the bandana tied around his wrist. The same red-and-white bandana that Bear had put on to keep his bandage in place.

He remembered it so clearly. How he'd cut his hand, and Bear had cleaned it up. How Bear had checked on it as they trekked through the jungle, and how he'd kept it above the river water as he crossed.

Omar studied his hand. The cut and the bandage were gone, just as if he had dreamed them.

But there was the bandana, tied around his wrist.

Omar felt his heart thud in his chest. He really had been on an adventure with Bear. Which meant he could get *back* to Bear.

How had he found his way to the jungle in the first place? He remembered getting lost, and – oh, yes. He had tried to use that trick compass.

Omar pulled the compass out of his pocket. It showed the usual four directions, but he distinctly remembered there had been five.

Then he stared. For a moment, the dial seemed to spin on its own and suddenly there were five directions again. At the same time there was a clattering noise as a can hit the trash can and bounced along the ground.

"Goal!" Chloe shouted to her

friend, and they laughed. Omar scowled. He remembered how Bear believed in taking care of the world around you. He knew Bear could teach Chloe a few useful things about that.

Omar looked back at the compass dial. There were just four directions again. But it had definitely been five ... just as Chloe had walked past.

Omar's eyes went wide.

Maybe it was that fifth direction. Maybe you couldn't find it.

It had to find you.

So Omar made a decision. Before going to apologize to Sophie, he had something to do.

It looked like Chloe was heading off

to some other activity, so Omar hurried forward and ducked in front of her.

"Hi?"

"Uh – hi."

Chloe slowed down and then stopped. She was staring at Omar with a look that said, *Do you need something*?

Omar thrust the compass at her before she could say anything. "I just wanted to give you this," he said.

She took it, smiling but clearly puzzled.

Omar tried to remember. What was it Sophie had said to him?

Oh, yes.

"Just consider it a gift," said Omar.

The End

Bear Grylls got the taste for adventure at a young age from his father, a former Royal Marine. After school, Bear joined the Reserve SAS, then went on to become one of the youngest people to ever climb Mount Everest, just two years after breaking his back in three places during a parachute jump.

Among other adventures he has led expeditions to the Arctic and the Antarctic, crossed oceans and set world records in skydiving and paragliding.

Bear is also a bestselling author and the host of television programs such as *Survival School* and *The Island*.

He has shared his survival skills with people all over the world, and has taken many famous movie stars and sports stars on adventures – and even President Barack Obama!

Bear Grylls is Chief Scout to the UK Scouting Association, encouraging young people to have great adventures, follow their dreams and to look after their friends.

Bear is also honorary Colonel to the Royal Marine Commandos.

When Bear's not traveling the world, he lives with his wife and three sons on a barge in London, or on an island off the coast of Wales.

Find out more at **www.beargrylls.com**